A King Production presents…

TOXIC SERIES

Sugar Babies…

A Titillating Tale

A Novelette

JOY DEJA KING

ISBN 13: 978-1958834992
ISBN 10: 1-958834-99-8
Cover concept by Joy Deja King
Library of Congress Cataloging-in-Publication Data;
A King Production
Sugar Babies...A Titillating Tale by Joy Deja King
Graphic design: www.anitaart79.wixsite.com/bookdesign
Typesetting: Anita J.

For complete Library of Congress Copyright info visit;
www.joydejaking.com
Twitter @joydejaking

A King Production
P.O. Box 912, Collierville, TN 38027
A King Production and the above portrayal log are trademarks of A King Production LLC

This Novelette is Dedicated To My:

Family, Readers, and Supporters.
I LOVE you guys so much. Please believe that!!

—Joy Deja King

A special THANK YOU to RG, for motivating me to get back to doing what I love. I will always adore you. For Life.

—Joy Deja King

A KING PRODUCTION

Sugar Babies...

Toxic
Series

A Titillating Tale

A Novelette

JOY DEJA KING

Chapter One

This Can't Be My Life

"You ungrateful bitch!" He spit in her face while gripping her neck as her legs dangled off the floor. His tone was sinister, and he had demons dancing in his eyes. "You thought I was going to let you leave me. It took time and knocking on a lot of doors, but I finally found you. I warned you not to fuck me over," he asserted before hurling her body against the wall.

"You're so sick," she uttered catching her breath. "I didn't fuck you over, you fucked yourself. I can't believe I ever thought I loved you," she cried as this predator slowly marched towards her. Fearing for her life, she grabbed the only thing within her reach to use as a potential weapon.

She swung the opalescent shimmer and smoke like swirl colored glass abstract sculpture, grazing the side of his head. The heavy figurine didn't make enough contact to do the damage she hoped but it did break the skin, causing a deep gash. The blood gushing from the laceration dripped into his eyes, making him disoriented long enough for her to use the opportunity to get away.

"I'ma kill you, you stupid bitch!" He roared as she sprinted across the room but before she reached the door the sound of gunshots brought everything to a halt.

Six Months Earlier...

"Where the fuck am I?" Paige mumbled, pulling the silk sheet over her face to keep the glaring sun peeking through the large bedroom window out of her eyes. Her head was throbbing, and the symptoms of a hangover was in full effect the morning after a night of heavy drinking. Paige should've been over waking up to sensitivity to light and sound, nausea, stomach pain, dizziness, pounding headache, dry mouth and excessive thirst but instead she continued her hard partying ways.

"So sorry! I didn't realize anyone was here," the cleaning lady exclaimed when she noticed a svelte body shifting under the sheets.

"What time is it?" Paige questioned in an almost inaudible voice.

"Excuse me?"

Paige flung the sheet from over her face, "What time is it?"

"One o'clock, Miss. I'll let you sleep," the cleaning lady said turning to walk out the bedroom door.

"Wait!" Paige called out. She let out a deep sigh and rubbed her eyes, as her mind became more lucid. She rose in bed, focusing on the woman standing in the entryway with a cleaning bag strapped around her shoulder and waist. "Rosita!" she said with enthusiasm, happy her memory was back.

"Good day, Miss Paige," Rosita smiled.

"Please be a doll and bring me a strong cup of coffee."

"Will do."

"Wait!" Paige called out, once again stopping Rosita. "Where's Fitz?"

"Mr. Fitz not here. He not here when I arrive."

"Okay, thanks," Paige said reaching over to retrieve her phone off the nightstand. "Fuck," she huffed seeing all the missed calls from her father. She then read the text message from Fitz.

Had to catch a flight to NY. Be back in a couple days. Call me when you wake up

Right when Paige was about to call Fitz, her father was calling again. "Hello."

"Why haven't you called me back, Paige?" her father asked in a stern voice.

"Good morning to you too, daddy," she exhaled, praying and making false promises to herself that she would never get drunk again if her head would stop thumping.

"Don't you mean good afternoon," he countered.

"Of course, so what's up?"

"What are you doing?"

"Getting ready to head to class," she said

mouthing *thank you* to Rosita after she handed her a cup of coffee. Paige was desperate for a boost of caffeine.

"Really? I find that interesting since you got a letter from the dean today."

"Letter, did you read it?"

"This is my house, of course I read it."

"What did it say?" Paige pretended to want to know although her preference was to end the phone call.

"You received an academic dismissal because of your poor grades. You were given an opportunity to appeal to the committee members, but instead you chose to voluntarily drop out," her father stated. "I want an explanation. What is going on with you?"

Fuck! I can't believe they sent that letter to my parent's house. I could've sworn I put the address to the condo down as the return address. This is some straight bullshit! Think! Think! Paige screamed to herself.

"Paige, did you hear me?"

"Yes, I heard you," she said taking a few sips of coffee, hoping it would magically give her brain some power to quickly come up with a plausible lie.

"Then answer the question. Why did you

drop out of school and when did you plan on telling us...or was that not part of your plan?" he demanded to know.

"Daddy, would you please calm down," Paige said sweetly.

"No, I will not calm down. You told me you were on your way to class, which was obviously a lie. You flunked out of school. Probably due to you following behind that idiotic youtuber boy!" He shouted.

"Daddy, I told you he is a music artist that so happens to have a YouTube channel...with millions of followers mind you," she shot back defensively.

"Since you're no longer in school, are you planning on getting a job to support yourself?"

"Excuse me?" she stuttered. Shocked by the question, Paige placed her cup on the nightstand before she spilled it all over herself.

"How are you going to support yourself, Paige? Do you plan on getting a job?"

"I guess, but when you say support do you mean groceries and stuff?"

"Groceries, rent, car note, car insurance..."

"Daddy, I just turned twenty. I seriously doubt I can find a job that will pay all my bills," she scoffed.

"When you got your condo and I bought you a new car, it was with the understanding you would be attending college."

"I might go back to school. Like a reverse gap year. Instead of taking a year off right after I graduated from high school, I'm taking it now," she reasoned.

"Fine Paige, but you'll be taking that so called gap year from here."

"What do you mean here...I have to move back to Maryland?"

"That's exactly what I mean. I will not continue to pay your bills in Los Angeles when you're not in school full time. You can figure out what you want to do with your life from your home here in Maryland with your mother and I."

"You can't be serious! That isn't fair. I have a life here, friends. I can't just up and leave and move back to Maryland. Please daddy. Just give me six months to find myself. If I don't go back to school, then I'll get a job. I promise. But until I decide, you can't cut me off financially. It wouldn't be fair."

Paige could tell her pleas had the intended effect on her father and he was contemplating what she said. He inhaled and exhaled deeply before speaking. "Well, I suppose..."

"Let me speak to her!" Paige could hear her mother say to her father while grabbing his phone. "Paige Elizabeth Langston." She knew when her mother said her full name the conversation wouldn't end well.

"Yes mother."

"Your father will not be giving you another dime except to buy you a plane ticket to Maryland, so stop asking him. Do you understand me?"

"Gail, give me back the phone. I need to finish my conversation with our daughter," her father said but her mother was not having it.

"No. The only conversation you're having is with me. Paige, you can start packing your belongings. I'll be in touch with your flight details," her mother said and ended the call.

Paige let out a high-pitched scream and threw her iPhone across the room. "This can't be my life!"

Chapter Two

No Way Out

"Are you fuckin' hard of hearing? That's not what I said Fitz. I don't wanna stay with you. I need you to give me some fuckin' money! Go fuck yourself you cheap fuck!" Paige screamed ending the call.

"What was that about?" Lydia muted the television and asked when her bestie came through the door yelling.

"Where do I even start." Paige slumped down

on the couch face first, wanting to bury her misery.

"You can start with why you were screaming at Fitz."

"I asked him for some money to pay next month's rent and he basically refused. Instead, he said I could crash at his crib...as if," Paige sneered rolling her eyes. "His stupid friends are always there. I can't even walk to the kitchen naked."

"Wait a second." Lydia moved over to the couch Paige was occupying. "Why do you need Fitz to pay your rent? I thought your father covered all your expenses."

"He does...I mean he did, up until he received the fuckin' letter from the dean saying I would no longer be attending the University."

"What! When did you stop attending school?" Lydia was glancing around completely perplexed.

"I was partying a bit too much with Fitz and missing some classes. Of course, my grades suffered, and I got an academic dismissal," she explained nonchalantly.

"I'm sure you can appeal it. They'll give you another chance Paige."

"They already gave me the opportunity, but I declined," she shrugged.

"Why would you do that and why didn't you tell me?" Lydia wanted to know. "I feel so out the loop."

"Does it really matter?" Paige was now facing Lydia. "I need to figure out how I'm going to pay this rent and the rest of my bills now that my father has cut me off financially," she said shaking her head. "If my mother would've just stayed out of it, he would've given me six months."

"So, what do they expect for you to do?"

"Move back to Maryland."

"If you move back to Maryland that means I have to find someplace else to live," Lydia sighed.

"I'm not moving back home with my parents. That will never happen. I just need to come up with some money until I can get a job."

"That's a bit ambitious don't you think? I mean you've been letting me live here rent free, which I greatly appreciate, especially under my current circumstances. But even if you got a full-time job and I gave you money from my part time job, I highly doubt it would put a dent in how much the rent is here. I get this place isn't one of those impressive mansions you grew up in, but this condo is pretty fancy. You would need one hell of a job to pay the rent here."

"I hear you, but I have two weeks to figure

it out," Paige huffed. "Sitting here wallowing is not doing me any favors, plus I'm hungry. Do you have a class to get to?"

"No, I'm done for the day."

"Good, then you can join me for a late lunch. My treat. Surely my dad hasn't cut off my credit cards yet. If he has, I hope you can cover the bill," Paige joked.

"Fingers crossed the credit card goes through because my funds are funny," Lydia laughed.

"I think we're good but, in the meantime, I'm going to take a shower and get dressed. I want to look extra cute just in case this is my last meal at an expensive restaurant," Paige winked.

Crimson's eyes remained fixated on the ceiling, where she stared at a damp stain in a cheap motel room her boyfriend, who was also her pimp rented by the hour. This was her sixth customer today, and it wasn't even midafternoon. Staring up at the ceiling was the only way she could escape her body, as the obese man pounded inside her dry pussy like she was a punching bag. After three minutes he made a loud grunting noise before rolling over on his back. He was breathing heavy with his ribbed white tank top drenched in sweat. Beating her pussy was probably the hardest workout the man had in many, many years.

"You can leave the other half of the money you owe on the table," Crimson said getting up from the bed and heading to the bathroom.

"I was thinking we could go at it one more time. I can feel my nature rising again," he snorted looking down at his shriveled penis with the condom still attached.

"You'll need to speak with Tony about that."

"But I paid for the hour."

"You get one sex act per booked session. It took you thirty minutes to get it up," Crimson released a heavy sigh. "Anything else will cost you extra."

"But..." before the man could complete his thought there was a loud knock at the door.

"Hey," Crimson said when she opened the door and saw Tony standing there. She knew it was him, as he was a stickler for time and the customer's hour had run out.

"Where's the money?" Tony wanted to know. Crimson glanced over at her customer who still had his dick out. "I need the rest of my money."

"Sure," he said reaching down on the floor for his pants to retrieve his wallet. "I was wanting to pay for an additional hour."

"Can't do it. Another customer will be here in ten minutes."

"I was hoping I could go get some food. I haven't eaten all day and I'm starving," Crimson complained wanting to put an end to her hunger cramps.

"Here, you can have this other burger I didn't finish eating," Tony said tossing the crumbled-up McDonald bag on the table.

"Thanks."

"Hurry up and eat, and go clean yourself up," Tony dictated. "Can't have you fuckin' up my money by making the customer wait," he griped.

Crimson jammed the few leftover bites of hamburger down her throat and went directly to the bathroom. She turned on the faucet, to take a bird bath, as she only had time to quickly wash her private parts and underarms. While cleaning herself, Crimson glanced up and caught her reflection in the mirror.

"What happened to you?" she mumbled, seeing the emptiness in her once alive hazel eyes.

Crimson was a sweet and naive fifteen-year-old, who was also neglected when she met Tony. She never knew her father and from the time she was a little girl, her mother changed boyfriends like most people change their underwear. This left Crimson feeling alone and unloved. She had no friends at school because although she was pretty, she always looked somewhat unkept. Her mother only worked dead end jobs, so they had little money. Whatever was left over, her mother spent on liquor.

Her life would be forever changed when one day when she was walking home from school, a guy driving a fancy convertible pulled up and introduced himself as Tony. Crimson figured this cute guy in an expensive car had to be lost and needed directions, because why else would he be talking to some stringy hair, poorly dressed, awkward teenage girl. To her surprise, Tony asked for her phone number, and he called her that same night. She was left home alone so often without any parental guidance; it was a breeze for Tony to step in and take complete control of Crimson's life.

Initially, Tony was taking Crimson out to eat, getting her hair done and buying her new clothes. For the first time in her life, she felt special and beautiful. People at school thought she was the new girl who transferred from another school. No one believed she was the mostly ignored, sometimes teased, Crimson Monroe who sat alone every day at lunch. Tony remained committed to his charade of being a dream boyfriend for months. He stole her virginity and soul all at once. By the time Crimson realized she had fallen in love with a diabolical predator she was in too deep.

Chapter Three

Out Of Options

Paige and Lydia were enjoying what they deemed to be their last expensive meal at the overpriced Gucci Osteria da Massimo Bottura, a ritzy restaurant from the luxury fashion house located in Beverly Hills. The elegant eatery was tucked above the Gucci store. Paige was tempted to make a few purchases at the designer boutique after their meal but didn't want to push her luck. She felt her mother would be canceling her credit cards at any moment and couldn't endure the embarrassment if her transaction was declined. But for the moment, she was living her best life as a privileged princess.

With her perfect facial symmetry, high cheekbones, rich brown skin, far apart alluring eyes, full pouty lips, and tall, slender body with a hint of seductive curves, made Paige Supermodel looks fit in perfectly with the upscale Italian vibe, that was casually elegant. There was bold print wallpaper, marble walls and marble mosaic floors. The intimate space was adorned with stunning floral arrangements, red tufted banquettes and pink cushions, and a few Gucci-print armchairs that provided a pop of branding.

"Maybe I should've stayed in school," Paige giggled as she sipped on one of their forty-dollar cocktails featuring Gucci imprinted ice cubes. "I'm not ready to give all this up."

"I feel you because I'm not ready to find a new place to live," Lydia exhaled. "I mean, I could never afford a condo like yours but until I get through medical school and can secure a medical residency, I might end up homeless. Working this part time job is already affecting my grades which is putting my scholarship in jeopardy. Why can't I have a rich daddy like you," she lamented.

"Would you ladies like to get anything else before you close out your check?" their waitress asked. "Maybe one of our desserts or perhaps another round of drinks."

"I'll leave that up to you," Lydia smiled. "I can only imagine how high the bill already is."

"No need to worry about the check. That gentleman over there," the waitress said pointing to a distinguished looking gentleman sitting alone at a table in the glass-enclosed terrace. "He's covering the cost." The man gave a slight smile and nodded his head.

"Wow!" Lydia grinned widely.

"Maybe you just found your daddy," Paige cracked, as the two friends burst out laughing.

"We'll definitely take another round of drinks and whatever desserts you recommend," Paige announced with enthusiasm.

"I'll be back shortly. Let me know if you ladies need anything else."

"We will," Paige smiled before the waitress walked off. "Here he comes," she uttered under her breath to Lydia, when she noticed the man heading their way.

"Good afternoon, ladies."

"Hi," the ladies said simultaneously.

"We appreciate you paying for our meal," Lydia beamed.

"Yeah, for sure," Paige added.

"My pleasure. I'm Grayson."

"I'm Paige."

"And I'm Lydia."

"It's nice to meet both of you. Paige, I know you're probably already taken, but if not, I would love to take you out to dinner."

Paige and Lydia eyed each other. "Thanks but..." Before Paige could decline the invite, Lydia discreetly kicked her leg under the table. "But I feel like I owe you dinner after you were so kind to cover our check," she said recovering like a pro.

"Then have dinner with me but you don't owe me anything."

"Sure," Paige agreed and the two exchanged numbers. "You didn't have to kick me so hard," she grumbled when Grayson left their table.

"You were about to mess things up. I had to save you from yourself."

"Excuse me?" Paige scoffed.

"He doesn't even know you and he's paying for what I can only imagine is our very expensive meals."

"And because of that he deserves a dinner

date?"

"You said he could be the rich daddy I was looking for, maybe he can be yours," Lydia proposed.

"That was a joke."

"I took you seriously and I'm not joking. When he came to our table, I was hoping he was interested in me. But with that body and your face, I should've known he wanted you."

"Oh please, you're gorgeous. Maybe he's just in the mood for some chocolate," Paige cackled. "Oh goodness, that's him calling me now," she said answering. "Hello."

"I know I just left but why wait. How about dinner tonight?"

"Why not, dinner tonight it is." Paige rolled her eyes as Lydia silently clapped her hands.

"I'll call you back in about an hour with the details," he said.

"Okay, I'll be looking out for your call."

"This is so exciting," Lydia gushed.

"I'm glad one of us thinks so."

"I think he's very handsome and obviously he's not short on cash."

"He's handsome but I'm not typically attracted to older white men," Paige clarified.

"I get it. I know you go for the hip hop type

guys, but desperate times can change your mind," Lydia reminded her.

Paige had been accustomed to having unlimited access to her father's funds for so long, she never considered dating men for money. That's why she was offended and shocked when Fitz refused to give her cash, she wasn't used to the word no but then again, she had never asked. But Lydia was right, things were different now. There was no way she was moving back home to live with her parents in Maryland, so if she wanted to stay and maintain her lavish lifestyle she needed to think outside the box. Maybe dating wealthy white men could be a suitable option.

"Crimson, hurry the fuck up!" Tony shouted grabbing his car keys off the kitchen counter. "Why the fuck aren't you dressed yet?" he barked when she came out the bathroom with a towel around her naked body.

"Tony, I'm not feeling well. When I got out the shower, I threw up. I really don't feel up to working today. I think I might be coming down with the flu or something," she said wanting to crawl back in the bed.

"My baby not feeling good," Tony said sounding concern, stroking the side of her face.

"No," Crimson shook her head. "I just want to get some rest."

"I don't give a fuck what you want!" He growled slamming the back of her head against the wall. Tony wrapped Crimson's long hair around his hand, gripping it tightly. "The only rest you'll be getting is on your back while serving your fuckin' customers, cunt."

"Tony, you're hurting me," Crimson cried out.

"You lucky I need yo' ass to get to work or I would put my fist in your mouth, so you can stop fuckin' whining. Now go get dressed, before I change my mind and beat the shit outta you!" He threatened.

Crimson did as she was told, making her way to the bathroom. Instead of getting back in the bed, she grabbed some Excedrin migraine from the cabinet to minimize the agonizing pain Tony had inflicted on her head. She wasn't sure how much longer she could deal with his abuse. Tony laying hands on Crimson had become more traumatic than the countless men running through her. She had almost become numb to the inconsequential sex she had with repulsive men on a daily basis but the physical and mental abuse she endured by a man she once believed loved her, had taken its toll.

Chapter Four

Seeking Arrangements

This was the third time within the last week that Paige was having dinner with Grayson. Although she enjoyed being wined and dined at all these fancy restaurants, rent would soon be due, so the luxury of time was not on her side. She needed to cut through the bullshit and get right to the point.

"Grayson, I've really been enjoying these dinner dates we've shared together. You've introduced me to some amazing restaurants I never knew existed."

"I've enjoyed our dinners together also and would love to introduce you to so much more. Not only are you exceptionally beautiful but also very witty. I truly enjoy your company Paige, and would like to see you even more," he asserted.

"How much...I mean how much more would you like to see me?" Paige asked unable to get her need for money off her mind.

"You tell me. I know you're young and I'm sure very busy with your friends, but I would like for you to make more time for me. I'm a business-man, so I recognize time is money. I can make it worth your while."

Oh snap, now he's speaking my money language. But how do I go about negotiating a price for my time. Since he's the businessman, maybe I should let him lead the financial discussion, Paige thought to herself.

"So, tell me Grayson, how much is it worth to you, to spend time with a girl like me?" Paige teased, playing with the strawberries and whip cream in the glass bowl.

"That can vary, depending on the type of time we spend with each other."

"I'm listening...tell me more," she said although she knew what type of time Grayson was alluding to.

"You know that I'm extremely attracted to you, and I believe we would enjoy having sex. But I also know that most times beautiful women enjoy beautiful gifts even more than sex, which I would love to shower you with."

"Here's the thing Grayson, yes I love beautiful gifts, but I also need money for my bills," Paige divulged, tired of taking the slow stroll to reach her end goal. "I'm taking some time off from school, so my parents have demanded I move back home, because my father will no longer be supporting me financially here in LA."

"That explains a lot."

"What do you mean?"

"I was wondering how you were able to afford to live so well, especially at such a young age. But this is LA and beautiful women like yourself do have options. I didn't want to pry but I would've never guessed a rich father was footing the bill."

"Yes, and honestly I want to stay in LA so it would be nice if you would take over those expenses."

"I see. It seems you're seeking for us to have some sort of arrangement...correct?" Grayson wanted validation.

"I suppose that's a fair interpretation. Is it something you're interested in or..."

"Very interested." Grayson stated cutting Paige off before she finished asking her question.

"I'm happy to hear it. When will this arrangement begin?"

"How about tonight. I can write the check right now."

"How about we start tonight, and you give me the cash, or we can start after the check clears. It's up to you," Paige smiled sweetly.

"If I didn't know better, I would think you were a professional at this. You certainly don't come across as a novice," he surmised.

"Not a professional, just a quick learner. So, which one is it, cash or check?"

"Cash it is," Grayson agreed. And just like that, during dinner and drinks at a swanky restaurant in Malibu, a deal was struck, and an arrangement was made.

Instead of studying for an upcoming exam, Lydia

was browsing platforms and gathering information on how to find a sugar daddy. Her exhaustive research led her to a website called Secret Benefits. It was supposed to be safer than any other website and extremely popular. Lydia had been fantasizing about securing the bag ever since her lunch with Paige. And once Paige started dating Grayson, Lydia believed her fantasy could become reality. Just like she had to study to become a doctor, Lydia put that same energy studying the dos and don'ts of catching a sugar daddy. The first thing she needed to do was set up an account on a sugar dating platform. The good news for Lydia was that most sugar dating platforms were free for sugar babies. Which was idyllic for a broke bitch like herself. Then she needed to upload some alluring photos and finally set her desired allowance.

Could those three simple steps really lead me to a life of lavish? Is it possible for me to find a rich sugar daddy while in the comfort of this condo on my laptop? These were questions Lydia was asking herself while debating if she should or shouldn't proceed. Her deliberation was interrupted when Paige came sauntering through the door without a trace of stress on her face.

"You seem to be in good mood," Lydia commented closing her laptop. "I haven't seen you this relaxed in a minute."

"A bitch done came into some money!" Paige boasted, kicking off her heels and tossing the wads of cash on the vintage coffee table.

"OMG! Bitch you better work! Grayson gave you all this money?!"

"You know it, in exchange for some of my goodies of course." Paige stuck out her tongue and laughed loudly.

"Unfreakin' believable. Now that you've gotten this money, are you going to see him again?"

"Of course. We have an arrangement. We spend time together and he pays my bills and buys me gifts."

"So, you're like a sugar baby!" Lydia proudly proclaimed.

"A what?"

"A sugar baby. A man who has a financial arrangement with a much younger woman is a sugar daddy and the woman is called a sugar baby," Lydia explained.

"Very interesting. I guess you're right. I'm now a proud member of the sugar baby gang," Paige enthused.

"You lucky bitch. You just walked right into the perfect arrangement, but I'm going to have to work for mine," Lydia exhaled deeply.

"Work for what?"

"I've been on this website trying to decide if I'm going to create an account so I can find me a sugar daddy," Lydia revealed opening her laptop and showing Paige the website.

"Wait, they have actual websites for this shit. Is it legit?"

"Very legit. This particular website comes highly recommended."

"What the fuck are you waiting for, join! I don't know how long this arrangement with Grayson will last. I'll feel a lot more confident with my situation if I have a backup option already in place."

"I don't know, I'm a little reluctant," Lydia admitted.

"Why, how much does it cost to join? I'll give you the money," Paige volunteered.

"No, it's actually free for potential sugar babies."

"Then what's the holdup? You're my bestie, so I never mind spending money on you, but wouldn't you rather have your own coins?"

"Yeah, of course but I'm not you Paige. What if I can't find a rich guy willing to give me a decent allowance."

"Girl stop! You're gorgeous. There will be plenty of sugar daddies looking to take care of your fine Asian ass. Okay...now what do we need to do to get yo' shit poppin'?" Paige questioned excitedly.

"I need to upload some pictures and set an allowance amount."

"That's it...oh bitch we got this. We about to get you cover magazine ready, take some sexy yet subtle pics and you'll be a member of the sugar baby gang before you know it. And we gon' spend that, spend that, spend that!" Paige bragged. "You ready to change your life?"

"I'm tired of being the broke medical student. I'm ready to spend that, spend that, spend that like you," Lydia chanted. "So yes I'm ready to change my life!"

"Then let's do it!"

Paige put on Drake's *Honestly, Nevermind*, poured them each a glass of her favorite wine, and the ladies spent the remainder of the evening getting Lydia dolled up, taking pictures and creating her sugar baby account. They were on a mission to find Lydia the perfect sugar daddy and by the end of the night, they were one step closer to doing exactly that.

Chapter Five

Change Of Plans

"Your father is booking your flight. Do you want to leave in the morning or afternoon?" Paige's mother asked.

"Neither."

"You have to choose morning or afternoon because they don't have any evening flights available."

"Mother, I don't need for you all to book me a flight because I'm not coming home," Paige stated flatly, while scanning her closet to decide what she was going to wear tonight.

"What do you mean, you're not coming home? If you're not coming home, then where are you going?"

"I'm staying here in LA?"

"You're moving in with that YouTube boy?" her mother mocked.

"I told you, he is a music artist, Geesh!" Paige smacked. "But no, I'm not moving in with Fitz. I'm staying here at my condo."

"Your father made it very clear that he will no longer be paying the rent at that condo, or any of your other bills since you flunked out of school."

"Mother, I remember the conversation vividly. I got a job and a roommate, so I'll be paying my own bills."

"Paying your own bills...you've never paid a bill in your entire life," her mother retorted.

"You all have left me no choice," she said coolly.

"Paige, what the hell are you talking about?" her father got on the phone and wanted to know.

"Put her on speaker phone," her mother shouted.

"Daddy, I got a job and a roommate to help

split the bills. I want to stay in LA until I figure out what I want to do with my life."

"What type of job?"

"With Amazon. They're hiring Air Hub Team Members. You're like in charge of making sure customers get their order on time. And you don't need any experience. Amazon will provide training," Paige informed her father as if she had applied and been hired for the legitimate job position. He wasn't sure how to respond.

"Enough of this clowning around, Paige."

"Daddy, I'm being serious. I got a job. You should be proud of me. I thought this is what you wanted. I mean isn't that the reason you completely cut me off financially?"

"Paige, that is not..."

"Phillip, don't allow her to run a guilt trip on you," her mother snapped, before her father could continue talking. "Paige doesn't have no damn job. When rent is due in a few days and she can't pay, trust me, she'll be calling begging for you to get her a flight home," she said confidently.

Dear Mother, if you only knew, Paige laughed to herself. *I already got my fuckin' rent money and the money for the rest of my bills too.*

"Daddy, I have to go. But don't worry about me. I'll be fine."

"Paige, just know I'll be here whenever you're ready to come home," her father stressed.

"Okay, daddy. Gotta go."

"You're not dressed yet!" Lydia stormed into Paige's bedroom looking polished in nude rib-knit pants with hip-cutouts, which she paired with a cream-colored zip-front maxi cardigan.

"I was on the phone being grilled by my parents," Paige frowned. "I'll be ready shortly. But you over there looking like an edible cutie. That outfit I picked out looks perfect on you," she raved.

"Don't I?!" Lydia agreed sounding shocked. "When you told me to get this outfit, I did not have high hopes. But since you were paying for it, who was I to complain," she laughed. "But I'm so glad I listened to you because I absolutely love this look!"

"So will the men at this sugar babies party tonight," Paige cheered.

"Speaking of the party, I'm so nervous," Lydia confessed.

"Why?"

"Because I'm basically putting myself out there hoping someone will choose me."

"In that outfit, you'll be doing the choosing. Those men are going to be tripping over each other trying to be your sugar daddy," Paige commented as she put on a baby blue front cowl cross satin mini dress. "Instead of being nervous, you should be thankful you created an account on that website. Because if you hadn't, you would've never gotten the invite to this exclusive party."

"True but I'm still nervous."

"Don't be, just enjoy the party and the free drinks of course," Paige suggested.

"That's easy for you to say. You've already secured a sugar daddy. Me, on the other hand, I've crossed over to desperation mode."

"I get you want to be able to buy yourself some fancy clothes and stuff, but that hardly warrants a need for desperation. I told you, you don't have to pay me any money to stay here. I got you covered," Paige reminded her friend.

"It's not just that. I lost my scholarship," Lydia disclosed. "If I want to stay in medical school, I'll have to pay the tuition myself."

"Oh shit! We are in desperation mode!" Paige declared. "No worries. I do my best work under pressure," she reassured Lydia, slipping on her slingback pumps. "Now let's get to this party. We have to secure you a sugar daddy."

Would you please hurry up, Crimson was saying to herself as the teenage boy humped on her like a rapid rabbit. He had to be all of nineteen years old and fucked like one who wasn't used to pussy. This was supposed to be her last customer after being holed up in some dusty, musty motel room all day and night. The quicker he got his shit off, the quicker Crimson could go home and get some much-needed sleep.

"That was awesome," the scrawny teenaged boy moaned after he was finally able to cum. He sat up in the bed and lit up a cigarette. "Would you like one," he offered taking a puff thinking he was a stud.

"No thanks," Crimson declined before reciting the standard statement Tony had drilled in her head. "You can leave the other half of the money you owe on the table."

"Sure, no problem."

Crimson went in the bathroom to take a quick shower and get dressed, so she was ready to go when Tony showed up. She knew he would be knocking on the door shortly which gave her a limited amount of time. The second she was coming out the bathroom, the customer was handing Tony the money on his way out the door.

"Why the fuck are you dressed?" Tony barked.

"You said he was the last customer."

"Shit done changed. You got one more," he announced.

"Tony, I'm exhausted. I can't do this again tonight," Crimson protested right as someone knocked on the door.

"Come on in," Tony told the man who resembled a married Sunday School Teacher instead of a horny guy paying for the services of a prostitute.

"Tony, can't he come back tomorrow? I've been here since eight o'clock this morning. I need to get some sleep."

"Oh no problem, I can come back tomorrow," the man nervously agreed.

"Don't listen to her, she works for me!" Tony snarled. "Now take yo' fuckin' clothes off and lay down."

Crimson reluctantly did as he said, not wanting to ignite his wrath.

"No, no. I'll come back tomorrow. You go get

some rest," the man said turning to leave.

"I said don't listen to her!" Tony shouted at the man.

"I just want to go," he replied seeming to regret his decision to buy some pussy.

"You ain't gettin' your deposit back," Tony spit.

"Keep it," the man said hurrying off.

"You dumb bitch! Look what you did!"

"Tony, you were able to keep the money. You didn't lose anything," Crimson said meekly.

"I lost the other fuckin' half he would've paid me if you had got on your back and let him fuck you," Tony roared with a backhand slap. Crimson pressed down on her cheek to lessen the sting.

"I'm sorry."

"Nah, you ain't sorry yet but you will be. Hurry up and put your clothes back on," he demanded.

Crimson knew what that meant. Tony was going to beat the brakes off her. He wanted to leave the motel to make sure no one was around to hear her cries, because all it took was one concerned citizen to call the police. She was dreading the ass whooping that was coming her way and wanted to avoid it at all cost.

Chapter Six

The Great Escape

When Paige and Lydia arrived at the exquisite home in the Hollywood Hills, they spent the first thirty minutes salivating on how gorgeous the place was. They imagined with all the retractable glass walls how it must have bathed the home in natural light during the day. On the lower level, there was a modern kitchen kitted out with high-end appliances and a dining room that opened onto a 200-square-foot private terrace. There was also a giant living room with a retractable wall that allowed you to turn the area into an outdoor loggia at the push of a button.

The free-floating metal staircase would lead you to a wood-lined office on the mezzanine and onto the upper floor. This level was dedicated entirely to the primary suite, which came complete with an elegant closet/dressing room. No detail was forgotten, mirrored cabinet doors inside the closets, velvet lined tables, charging stations for small appliances, a chandelier, and polished chrome accents that added to the sensation of opulence. The contemporary design lent a clean, modern aesthetic to the space. With a custom vanity table to do your hair and makeup, rotating glass shoe shelves, touch latch on all doors, 3000k warm white closet lighting, and a glass enclosed purse storage and even a mannequin to display your favorite jewels.

"Gurl! I could live in this freakin' closet and be perfectly content," Paige professed.

"Me too," Lydia nodded as she wandered off while Paige continued touring the home. All the bathrooms had heated Terrazzo floors, while walnut millwork and Corian was found elsewhere throughout. The real highlight was the glass, which was a work of art. The inspiration came from the paintings of Piet Mondrian, some windows had sections that were tinted with gold and silver. The surfaces were also treated for UV protection and set to optimize sunlight throughout different times of the day. All the windows were also equipped with automatic shades and specialized cooling/heating systems to keep the temp just right.

"What a masterpiece," Paige gasped.

"Thank you. I put a lot of thought into designing this place," the man stated arrogantly.

"Well, you have exquisite taste because your home is beyond magnificent," Paige said looking up at the man who appeared to be Nigerian.

"I saw you come in, are you enjoying the party?"

"To be honest, I've spent the majority of time walking through your house, admiring how beautiful it is."

"So, I'm assuming you haven't had the opportunity to meet any of the other men here?"

"No, but I'm not looking for a sugar daddy, I already have one. I came to support my friend," Paige said waving at Lydia who was doing some casual chatting with a small group of men.

"I see. I find it interesting that you don't have

a problem acknowledging you have a sugar daddy."

"Why would I? We're two consenting adults that have an arrangement we find mutually beneficial," Paige rationalized.

"You're refreshing."

"I don't think I've ever been described that way before but thank you."

"I'm Emmanuel," he extended his hand.

"I'm Paige." She returned the gesture and shook his hand.

"Paige, I would like to make you an offer. I want to put you under a three-month contract. After the three months, if we are both satisfied, we can extend it."

"I appreciate your candor. But as I stated, I already have an arrangement in place. I don't think I would be able to juggle both of you."

"That would not be allowed under our contract anyway. Name your price."

"Even if I wanted to, I couldn't. He has already paid me for the upcoming month."

"I'll reimburse you the money to give back to him."

"You'll give me the money to pay my current sugar daddy back and I can name my price for our three-month contract?"

"Yes. Do we have a deal?"

Paige was intrigued. But the deal almost seemed too good to be true. She wanted to bite but then she had to consider that the man might be bullshitting her. With Grayson she knew he was a sure thing, at least for now. This Emmanuel man could be a fraud. In fact, what if this incredible house wasn't even his. Her head was spinning weighing the pros and the cons.

"I don't know," Paige hesitated. "It's a tempting offer but..."

"But what?" he pressed Paige for an answer. "Tell me why you won't accept my offer."

"I just don't feel comfortable giving you an answer right now."

"Take my business card. Once you have a chance to consider my proposition, give me a call."

"Sure." Paige took the business card. She was drawn to his straightforwardness and confidence. If his money was right like he portrayed, Paige was prepared to trade in her current sugar daddy for a more lucrative arrangement.

"Omigosh! This party was fuckin' incredible!" Lydia screamed when they got back in the car. "I can't believe I actually considered not coming."

"Seriously? You told me you were nervous but never that you considered not attending the party." Paige was shocked.

"Yeah, I didn't want you to tease me," she laughed. "But it worked out better than I ever imagined. I met four potential sugar daddies," Lydia said with glee.

"I told you this would be your night," Paige snapped her fingers turning up the volume on the radio.

"You were right. I'm going to weigh my options, maybe have lunch or dinner with each one before making my decision."

"I think that's a smart move. Although this is a paid arrangement, ideally you want to choose the man you have the most chemistry with."

"Exactly!" Lydia yelled applauding herself for doing what she perceived to be a strategic move. "Umm, where are you going?" she asked once she looked out the window and realized nothing looked familiar.

"Damn, I missed my turn," Paige sighed. "Let me turn around." After driving around for fifteen minutes they were now completely lost.

"I don't know why you didn't just put your

address in the GPS," Lydia shrugged.

"For some reason I thought I could figure it out. I guess the alcohol is playing tricks on me. But let me run in this convenience store and use the restroom before I piss on myself," Paige said parking her car.

"I'm right behind you because I have to go too."

As Paige was getting out the car, Emmanuel's business card fell out her purse. When she spotted it laying on the ground, she felt her heart was about to stop. *What if I hadn't noticed the card dropped out my purse, I would've lost his number. Any chance of seeing him again would be impossible,* she thought to herself. It wasn't until that very moment did Paige realize she didn't want to take that risk.

"You keep whining about needing some sleep. Well guess what," Tony said clutching underneath Crimson's chin, turning her face towards him. "After I beat the shit outta you, you'll be so bruised and battered, you'll need to take off at least a week to fully recover."

"Tony, I said I was sorry. I'll never complain again," she promised.

"Too late. You should've thought about that shit before you embarrassed me in front of a customer. But I'ma teach you a lesson tonight that you'll never forget."

Crimson swallowed hard, cringing at thought of what was going to happen to her once they got home.

"Tony, if I can't work for a week, I won't be able to make you any money," she said hoping his thirst for cash would convince him not to put her out of commission by beating her until she was black and blue.

"You ain't gotta worry about that. While you at home getting all that rest you been dying for, I'ma break this new bitch in. Put her ass to work. Once you done licking yo' wounds and you can cover up them bruises with some makeup, I'll put you back to work. Then I'll have two hoes out here making me some fuckin' money," Tony hyped.

Crimson imagined the pain that would soon be inflicted on her at the hands of Tony and knew it was time to make an escape. When they pulled up to the traffic light, they were sandwiched between a car in the front of them and one in the back. Her heart was racing. She wanted to make a run for it but was paralyzed with fear. The only thing that she feared more was the brutality she would soon face if she didn't get away. That gave Crimson the strength to jump out the car and run for her life.

She could hear Tony threatening to kill her while yelling she was a dumb hoe as she kept running determined not to look back. Crimson had no idea where she was. She ran down a residential street before seeing a convenience store a block away. She was huffing and puffing, wanting to stop for a moment and catch her breath, but she pushed through until she reached the store.

"Please help! My boyfriend is trying to kill me," Crimson cried falling into Paige's arms as she was walking out the store.

"Dear God, I need to get you some help," Paige said staring at the woman who was barefoot, breathing heavy with a bruise on her cheek. It was obvious she had been through a traumatic experience.

"I had a craving for a candy bar," Lydia said coming out the store. "I got you one too," she continued, biting down on a Twix unaware of what was going on until she saw Paige's arm around a young woman who wasn't wearing any shoes. "Who is she?"

"I don't know but she needs our help," Paige said walking over to her car and helping the young woman inside. In Paige's arm, Crimson felt like a fragile bird on the verge of losing her wings. "Are you hungry...can I get you anything?"

"No." Crimson shook her head, eyes wide with fear.

"You don't have to be scared. You're safe now." Paige wanted to calm the frightened woman.

"Can someone tell me what happened?" Lydia questioned sitting in the backseat completely confused.

Paige was about to explain what little she knew but got distracted when a car pulled up with their high beam lights flooding the parking lot. Crimson turned and immediately recognized the vehicle.

"It's him." Crimson's entire body started shaking uncontrollably.

"Get down." Paige pushed Crimson's body down in the passenger seat. Luckily, she had tint as the man pulled up right next to her. When he stepped out his car, he had a menacing presence. Tony turned and stared directly at Paige. She pretended not to notice him eyeing her Benz with intensity as if he knew his prey had found refuge inside her car.

"He looks scary. I think we should get the hell out of here. Like right now!" Lydia urged.

"I agree but he's staring awfully hard, so I don't want to come off suspicious." Paige exhaled wanting to keep her cool, especially after glancing down at Crimson and seeing that her hysterical shaking had yet to stop. Tony was standing in front of the convenience store, seeming to want his presence known. His demonic eyes darted around the parking lot determined to locate what he considered to be his missing personal property. After five more minutes Tony finally went inside the store. That's when Paige used the opportunity to drive off, freeing Crimson from the grasp of her sadistic boyfriend for the first time in years.

Chapter Seven

Unbreakable

"Wait until I tell you about my lunch date today!" Lydia came parading through the door eager to give Paige all the details.

"Keep your voice down. Crimson is still sleeping." Paige put her index finger over her mouth signaling Lydia to speak softly.

"Crimson?" Lydia looked puzzle.

"The girl we brought home last night."

"Oh, so she finally told you her name?"

"Yeah. She woke up this morning after you left for class. We talked briefly and then she went back to bed. I don't think the poor girl has had a good night sleep in months."

"How long are you planning on letting her stay here?" Lydia sat down on the couch next to Paige. "I mean do you think it's wise to keep her here?" she asked not masking her concern.

"I didn't ask her how long she wanted to stay and I'm not rushing her to leave. It's not like we don't have the space. We never even use that third bedroom."

"So, what you're going to let Crimson be the third roommate? I think you need to slow down, Paige."

"I didn't say she was going to be our room-mate," Paige huffed. "Crimson may not even want to stay here with us, but I don't mind if she does. She seems sweet to me."

"Maybe she is sweet, but did you see that boyfriend of hers. He looked like a monster."

"Which is why she needs our help."

"I never pictured you as the save the world type," Lydia cracked.

"I'm not, but there's just something about her. When she ran up to me at the convenience store, I had never seen someone so vulnerable and fragile. It just had an unexpected effect on me," Paige professed.

"Oh no, you've turned into a bleeding heart. Aren't I the one who is supposed to be in medical school, so one day I can save lives, or is that your role now?" she taunted.

"Enough of this, tell me about your lunch."

"Yes! I went to lunch with Jeff, and it was amazing!" Lydia's eyes lit up.

"He's one of the potential sugar daddies you met at the party last night?"

"Yes, and the crazy part is he was the one I thought I would like the least. He agreed to the monthly allowance I requested, and his terms are super reasonable."

"So, you're not going to meet with the other men?"

"I'm supposed to have dinner with another man tonight, so it would only be fair that I go out with the other two before I make my final decision."

"Speaking of decisions, I need to call Emmanuel," Paige remembered.

"Who is that?"

"You know that man I was speaking to when you were over there chatting it up with those guys."

"You mean the man that owns the house where they had the party last night?"

"How do you know that?" Paige was curious to find out.

"When you waved at me, one of the guys I was talking to, mentioned the man you were standing near was the owner of that fuckin' fabulous crib," Lydia explained.

"Wow, and I doubted him when he told me that."

"Wait, that's the Emmanuel you need to call?"

"Yes indeed."

"Is he trying to be your sugar daddy?"

"Sure is."

"You have to be the luckiest bitch ever," Lydia shook her head. "You haven't agreed to do it?"

"Not yet."

'What the fuck are you waiting for? That man has to be loaded."

"Seems to be but..." Paige stopped talking when she saw Crimson coming down the hallway. "Good afternoon!" She greeted her cheerfully.

"Hey! What time is it? I felt like I've been sleeping all day."

"Technically you have. It's after four," Paige

informed her. "But you clearly needed the rest and I'm glad you got it."

"Hi Crimson. Not sure if you remember me but I'm Lydia," she said getting up to get a closer look at her.

"Yes, I remember you," she nodded.

"Do you live around here?" Lydia pried.

"Oh no, I could never afford to live over here." Crimson's eyes widened.

"I didn't mean in this exact neighborhood, but you know in the LA area."

"Oh yeah, I grew up in LA."

"Really...how old are you and are you still in school?"

"She just woke up. You don't need to interrogate her." Paige cut her eyes at Lydia.

"It's okay, I just turned nineteen. And I dropped out of school." Crimson put her head down as if embarrassed.

"Then we have something in common because I dropped out of school too." Paige jumped up from the couch and walked over to Crimson taking her hand. It was obvious Paige was protective of the woman who wasn't much younger than her.

"I doubt you dropped out of high school," Crimson slightly smiled.

"No but it doesn't matter, we're both still theoretically dropouts." They shared in the humor of it all. "Are you hungry? Some food I ordered just got here. I wasn't sure what you liked, so I just got a variety of stuff."

"Yes, I'm starving."

"Then let's eat!" Paige led Crimson to the kitchen and Lydia lingered behind them sizing the woman up.

When they got to the kitchen, before she even sat down, Crimson started munching down her food.

"Goodness, she really was starving," Lydia whispered in Paige's ear.

"Let me pour you some juice," Paige offered thinking that as fast as Crimson was eating, she would need something to wash it down with. Crimson simply nodded her head yes because her mouth was full of food.

Lydia was anxious to continue her probing, but she recognized that Crimson's voracious appetite was unusual and made her pause. Also, seeing her in the brightly lit kitchen, Lydia noticed that she was on the skinnier side but not the sort of skinny that was purposeful more so forced. It made her wonder what sort of monster Crimson was running away from last night.

"Thank you so much for the food. I'm sorry, I feel like I ate so much, and I didn't leave much for you all," Crimson conceded when they sat down in the living room. But her food intake wasn't over. She was now eating the rest of the gelato Paige had in the freezer.

"No worries. Lydia just got back from a lunch date, and I really wasn't hungry."

"I still appreciate all the food. I guess it was obvious that I was starving. I also wanted to thank you for saving my life last night. I meant to tell you when I woke up briefly this morning and we spoke, but my mind was still in a daze. It's amazing what a goodnight sleep and some food can do," Crimson smiled. It was the first time she remembered authentically smiling in years.

"I'm just glad I was there to help."

"How long have you been with your boyfriend?" Lydia asked.

"Since I was fifteen."

"That's a long time. He seems a lot older than you," Paige remarked.

"He is. When I first met Tony, I couldn't believe this older cute guy was interested in me but in time I realized why." Crimson put her head down, sadness creeping from her face.

Paige and Lydia looked at each other, seeming to silently ask each other the same question until Lydia asked it out loud.

"Why was he interested in you?"

"You don't have to answer Lydia's question. We understand if you don't feel comfortable sharing something that is obviously hurtful for you," Paige said sympathetic to Crimson's pain.

"Tony was a boyfriend in disguise. He turned out to be a pimp."

"A pimp...what? Does that have anything to do with why you thought he was going to kill you?" Paige was now starting to feel like she was being intrusive, but she couldn't help herself. Her interest had been sparked and she wanted to know everything.

"Yes," Crimson nodded. "When I first met Tony, he made me feel special, like I mattered. I never knew my father and my mother was basically absent from my life, plus I didn't have any friends."

"That's really sad," Lydia said now feeling like a crummy person for ever thinking Paige needed to drop Crimson back off where they picked her up from.

"Well, as sad as that sounds, it was a dream life compared to the nightmare I've been living for the last few years. After months of Tony showering me with attention and gifts, he said I owed him. At first, I didn't know what he meant. Being dumb I thought he meant I owed him my heart, but I was already in love with him, so he had that."

"You weren't dumb, you were young and trusting," Paige articulated.

"Whatever the reason, falling in love with Tony was the worst mistake of my life. When he said owed, he meant I owed him back all the money he spent on me."

"How did he expect for you to pay him back?" Lydia leaned forward anticipating the answer to her question.

"He put me to work. For the last three years I've been somewhere in a seedy motel servicing different men and giving all my money to Tony."

Crimson's admission left Paige and Lydia with their mouths wide open with no words coming out. They were speechless. This was not the sad twisted love story they were expecting to hear, it was so much worse.

"He pimped you out." Paige stated the obvious in disbelief and horror.

"Yeah, and I remember the first time so explicitly. I thought we were going out to celebrate my sweet sixteen birthday but instead Tony beat me and made me have sex with some disgusting man. He described it as breaking me in." Tears began to trickle down Crimson's face with her confession. "And that's exactly what he accomplished that night, he broke my spirit and my soul. Being away from Tony is the first time I've felt free in years," she sobbed.

Paige and Lydia both went over to the chair where Crimson was sitting to console her.

"You are free of him. You never have to be bothered with a monster like Tony again. You're no longer alone, Crimson. You have me. I'm your friend," Paige assured her.

"You have me too," Lydia added wrapping her arm around Crimson. The three women all hugged each other, forming a bond that would prove to be unbreakable.

Chapter Eight

Survive The Night

Within the last few months, Paige, Lydia and Crimson had become inseparable. Having friends that were there to support her gave Crimson the strength to begin her journey of healing from all the emotional scars she'd buried. Paige and Lydia guiding her through that journey cemented what had become more than a friendship, they were more like a small tight knit family.

"Where are you off to in such a hurry?" Paige

questioned when saw Lydia frantically searching for something.

"I don't want to be late for my date with Jeff, but I can't find my car keys," Lydia complained.

"You can take my car," Paige offered.

"Found them!" Lydia announced. "But thanks for the offer."

"How are things going with Jeff anyway? I haven't heard you mention him lately."

"Great. He's a sweetheart. I just didn't realize how hard it would be juggling two sugar daddies and today I'm actually seeing them both," Lydia divulged.

"Maybe you should cut one off."

"Bitch, you better be joking. Between the allowance and other perks, I get from both men, life is fuckin' great!"

"I just don't want you stressed out. You're also in medical school. That's a lot to manage."

"I'll admit it's been difficult juggling both men and school, with the latter no longer being a priority."

"But initially paying for medical school was your motivation for getting a sugar daddy."

"I know but I'm making so much money and having so much fun, I'm starting to wonder if medical school is even worth the stress. But we can discuss this later. I can't keep Jeff waiting. Don't wait up!" Lydia said blowing Paige kisses on her way out the door.

"Did I just hear Lydia leave?" Crimson questioned coming into the living room.

"Yes, she's off to see her sugar daddy."

"And what about you, when is the next time you're going to see Emmanuel?"

"Not until this weekend."

"You don't sound very excited."

"Well, being a sugar baby is more like a financially lucrative business arrangement for me, although Emmanuel is my ideal sugar daddy. Our personalities seem to mesh perfectly. But clearly Lydia is having some next level enjoyment with her sugar daddies, so much so she doesn't seem to care about medical school any longer."

"Wow, I can only imagine how hard medical school is. Maybe Lydia just needs a little mental break from the stress that sometimes comes with being in school."

"Maybe, who knows but I must admit this is the happiest I've seen her. She loves being a sugar baby."

"I think I'm ready to create my sugar baby account."

"Are you sure?"

"I know you were concerned because of what I went through with Tony and being pimped out by him, but this would be different. I get to decide who I want to be with. I would be in control."

"True this is definitely different."

"Plus, it's time for me to make my own money. You and Lydia have been beyond generous, but I want to start paying my own way."

"I told you not to worry about money. You've been focusing on getting your GED and more importantly healing."

"And I do feel healed. Of course, not completely, but I've practically completely erased Tony's face from my memories and the nightmares are gone."

"That's the best news I've heard all week," Paige said giving Crimson a hug.

"Does that mean you'll help me create my account?"

"Of course. I did it for Lydia and I would love to do it for you. When do you want to get started?"

"I'm ready whenever you are."

"Then let's get started right now!" Paige beamed excited to get Crimson all dolled up. As she did with Lydia, she chose three different outfits. The sexy vixen, the girl next store and a leisure athletic look.

"You're really good at this," Crimson commented while Paige was putting the finishing touches on her hair and makeup.

"I've always loved the whole styling process, but I was used to doing it on myself. But doing it for you and Lydia, I realize I love styling other people even more."

"Can't you have a career doing that?"

"You mean like a stylist?" Paige asked.

"Yeah! Have you ever thought about being a professional stylist? I think you would be remarkable at it. I'm looking at myself in the mirror right now and I've never felt this beautiful."

"You are beautiful Crimson, and you look healthy."

"Thank you but what I'm talking about is my makeup and hair. I look glamourous and that's all you Paige. You really should consider being a stylist. I think you would be super successful."

"I might consider it but right now we need to focus on you. Now go get dressed we have some photos to take."

"This feels so fuckin' amazing," Jeff moaned pressing down on Lydia's head. He loved getting head even more than pussy and to Jeff, nobody gave a better blowjob than Lydia which was the reason she was his favorite sugar baby. "You're incredible," he groaned ejaculating in her mouth.

The first time Lydia gave Jeff a blowjob, when he ejaculated in her mouth, her first instinct was to spit it out. Jeff did nothing to disguise his disappointment and Lydia did nothing to hide the fact that it disgusted her. But when he told her he would pay her what he labeled a thousand dollar bonus each time she swallowed his cum, she learned to turn that disgust into bankable pleasure. On some of her visits when she spent the night with Jeff, she was leaving with an extra three thousand dollars which didn't include her monthly allowance. To Lydia, the money was too good to pass up.

"I'll be right back," Lydia said going to the bathroom to brush and gargle with mouthwash. Besides the money, sticking to this oral hygiene regimen made swallowing cum tolerable for her. She fixed her hair, which she had tied up in a sleek high ponytail. Once done, Lydia went back in the bedroom to collect her money and get dressed so she could leave.

"I wanted you to spend the night," Jeff said still sitting on the bed.

"Remember I told you yesterday I couldn't spend the night," Lydia reminded him.

Jeff watched as Lydia slipped on a backless red sundress with an airy skirt and a tight bodice, which featured a halter neckline and a deep V-cut. She paired the dress with minimal accessories, opting for red heels and diamond stud earrings he gifted her.

"But you never told me why."

"You didn't ask," she smiled sweetly.

"I'm asking you now. Why can't you spend the night?"

"I have to attend a dinner party for my girlfriend."

"How dare you lie to me."

"Jeff, what are you talking about? I'm not lying."

"You got a text from somebody named Dustin when you were in the bathroom." He said holding up her phone. "He can't wait to see you tonight."

"Jeff, when I was making my decision about getting a sugar daddy, I asked if you would have a problem with me having more than one and you said no."

"But it shouldn't interfere with the time we have scheduled together."

"Today was not our normally scheduled day. That is the reason I told you I wouldn't be able to spend the night before I agreed to see you. You said that was fine."

"That's before I found out you were going to see another man."

"It doesn't matter. Per our agreement, that should not be an issue for you."

"Well, it is. I don't want you seeing Dustin or any other man until our arrangement is over," Jeff stated.

"We can discuss this later. Please give me my money and phone so I can go," Lydia said grabbing her purse and reaching out her hand to Jeff.

"I can pay you extra."

"Jeff, we can discuss this later. Right now, I have to go," Lydia huffed becoming frustrated.

Without warning, Jeff flung Lydia's phone striking the side of her face. She lost her balance and fell back on the floor. Jeff jumped on top of her and wrapped his hands around her neck.

Lydia was struggling to breathe and trying to remain calm at the same time. She was hoping he would regain some self-control and stop choking her, but Jeff had completely snapped. She was feeling around for her purse and luckily, she was carrying an open tote bag.

Lydia grabbed her pepper spray and doused Jeff's face until the full effects kicked in. The chemical compound irritated his eyes, causing a burning sensation, pain and temporary blindness by dilating the eyes' capillaries and inflaming mucus membranes. In addition to affecting the eyes, it also inflames mucus membranes in the nose, throat, and lungs, causing breathing difficulties and a runny nose. The effects of the pepper spray can last up to 24 hours, but your target is only left blind for approximately fifteen minutes. Being aware of this, Lydia knew she needed to act fast and get the hell out.

"You'll pay for this; you piece of shit!" Lydia screamed, taking her heel and stomping Jeff in his stomach as he struggled to gain his composure. She grabbed her purse, phone and all the money he had on top of his dresser. Lydia ran out thankful she survived the night.

Chapter Nine

Warm Embrace

"I could get used to this." Paige stated in her typical cool, confident demeanor, sipping on vintage champagne while having dinner with Emmanuel on his superyacht.

"I'll admit you appear to be very comfortable as if you were born to live in opulence," Emmanuel observed.

"And I believe you're absolutely right," she beamed with eyes sparkling. Paige lifted her glass, "Let's cheer to that!" They clicked their glasses and she leaned over giving him a kiss.

"I love the way your lips feel against mine," Emmanuel said, leaning in for one more kiss.

"You always say that."

"Because it's true. I've enjoyed our last few months together."

"Who would've thought when we first met, that our three-month arrangement would turn into three more. In a few days we'll be creeping up on the six-month mark," Paige advised.

"I know. I'm pleasantly surprised. Usually, I get bored with my sugar babies, that's why I start them off on a three-month contract. You are the very first one I have ever done a six-months with," he disclosed.

"Is this your way of politely telling me you've become bored with my services and my contract will not be renewed?"

"I'm sure you're aware that there isn't a man alive who would become bored with you. Part of your appeal is the shroud of mystic that surrounds you. But again, you're aware of this."

"Does this mean you would like to extend our contract for another three months?" Paige got straight to the point. With every extension there was a bump in her allowance and she was ready to begin the negotiation process.

"Yes, I would like to extend our contract," Emmanuel confirmed.

"For how long, another three months or are we being ambitious and going for the full six?" she teased.

"I was thinking more along the line of indefinitely."

Paige almost spit out her last sip of champagne. "Is this a joke?"

"I don't joke about contracts." Emmanuel reached in his pocket and pulled out the most gorgeous diamond ring Paige had ever seen.

"Is that what I think it is?" Her heart felt like it was racing.

"That depends on your answer. You know I'm not the bended knee type. Besides nothing about our relationship has been conventional so why should my marriage proposal be any other way. I want you to be my wife, Paige. You excite me and hold my attention unlike any other woman I've ever known. You are remarkably beautiful. You have a face I would love to always wake up to. As you know I've dealt with my share of women, all types, so I know what I want, and I want you to be my wife. Will you marry me, Paige?"

"Of course, I can't think of a man who is more

fitting to be my husband. But you already know our prenup negotiations are going to be tough because I'm asking for everything.

"I wouldn't expect anything less from my future bride."

Paige and Emmanuel made love right there on the main deck of the yacht, disregarding the numerous bedrooms they had access to. It was probably their most impromptu sex session but with similar intensity. Their relationship was unique, and no doubt so would their marriage, but it worked for them. Paige's cool, confident and indifferent attitude was the perfect remedy for Emmanuel's arrogance. Paige was the trophy wife he had always envisioned, and Emmanuel was the optimal wealthy man who would supersede the lavish lifestyle her father made her accustomed to.

By the time Paige got home it was late, but she was still beaming over her engagement to Emmanuel. She admired the massive rock on her fourth finger one more time before opening the front door. She knew Crimson wasn't feeling well and had gone to bed early. She was trying to be as quiet as possible not wanting to wake her up. Upon entering her condo, Paige took off her heels, so they wouldn't be clicking against the hardwood floor. As she headed towards the living room an eerie feeling consumed her. She began to walk slower and suddenly stopped when she heard voices. One sounded like a man, and it was very intense. Paige reached for the gun she had in her purse, preparing for the unforeseen.

After the disturbing incident Lydia faced with her crazy sugar daddy Jeff a few weeks ago, Paige made sure to get protection. She now always carried a small pistol because there was no telling when you might need a weapon. Tonight, proved to be one of those times that having a gun would save a life. She walked in her living room and immediately recognized the monster standing several feet away. It was all happening so fast. Tony tossed Crimson across the living room with her body violently hitting the wall.

"You're so sick," Crimson uttered catching her breath. "I didn't fuck you over, you fucked yourself. I can't believe I ever thought I loved you," she cried. When Tony came over to render more damage, Crimson picked up the heavy figurine swinging it towards his head. There was blood and he appeared taken aback but he incurred minimal harm. However, it allowed Crimson the opportunity to run, and she ran right towards the warm embrace of her best friend's arms.

Paige knew this was the moment to make her move. She took full advantage of her fully loaded 9mm, pulling the trigger, making sure to penetrate her target and take him out permanently. Two bullets to the chest and one to the dome ensured Paige would be granted her wish.

"You don't have to shed another tear for that demon. He's dead," Paige promised holding Crimson closely.

Epilogue...

"You have to be the most beautiful bride I've ever seen," Lydia enthused.

"She's absolutely right. You look like an angel here on earth. Simply radiant," Crimson agreed, admiring the woman she loved like a sister.

"Both of you stop!" Paige said putting on a tad more lipstick and a dab of gloss.

"Only Paige would have an entire team of makeup and hair people at her disposable but would insist on putting the final touches on her lipstick," Lydia joked.

"Nobody knows my lips better than me," Paige nodded knowingly. "But wait, I have to ask, am I the only one who still can't believe I'm actually getting married!" she exclaimed filled with a flurry of emotions.

"No." Lydia and Crimson echoed in unison.

"I don't think I've accepted I'm losing my best friend," Lydia said somberly.

"Don't you dare say that. Our bond will never be broken. I think we've proven that we will always have each other's back," Paige said holding both of their hands.

"She's right. I always felt like I was alone in this world until I met the two of you. You all are my family. I would do anything for both of you," Crimson said squeezing their hands.

"You've shown that. When you called 911 you didn't have to tell them that it was you who shot Tony instead of me."

"It was the right thing to do. I brought that monster into your life. I should've been the one to take him out. So maybe I didn't actually pull the trigger, but in my mind that night I killed him. Remember that next day after I met you, I thanked you for saving my life, well you literally have, not once but twice. The least I could do was make sure you were never charged or investigated for his murder. I truly love and respect you." Crimson spoke from the bottom of her heart.

"I said I wasn't going to cry," Paige said using her hands to fan her face determined not to let one tear fall.

"I love you ladies so much," Paige embraced her best friends holding them tightly. "I'm proud of both of you. Crimson, thank God after their investigation the police ruled you shot Tony in self-defense, and you were never charged. Not only that, but you also received your GED, enrolled in college and even found a great sugar daddy to fund it all.

And my day one Lydia, you literally made Jeff pay for putting his hands on you. The financial settlement your attorney reached with him made it possible for you to finance medical school and focus on graduating. Because I know in my heart, you're meant to be a doctor and you're going to be a damn good one too! You all are the most incredible friends anyone could ever ask for. I'll soon be taking a new path as a married woman but my love for you both will never change," she vowed.

Paige, Lydia and Crimson came from different walks of life but the journey they each took would forever bond them. The trials and tribulations they shared had formed a friendship that would last a lifetime.

A KING PRODUCTION

Bitch

The Beginning...

Joy Deja King

Can't Knock the Hustle

Coming from nothing and having nothing are two dif ferent things. Yeah, I came from nothing, but I was determined to have it all. And how couldn't I?

I exploded into this world when "Hood Rich" wasn't an afterthought, but the only thought. You turn on the televi sion and every nigga is iced out with an exotic whip sit ting on 24inch rims, surrounded by a bitch in a gstring, a weave down to her ass, poppin' that booty. So the chicks on the videos were dropping it like it's hot for the rappers and singers while the bitches around my way were dropping it for our own superstars. Dealing with a street nigga on say the Alpo status a legendary drug kingpin was like being Beyoncé herself on Jigga Man's arm.

A bitch like me was thirsty for that. I'd been on some type of hustle since I was in Pampers.

I grew up in the grimiest Brooklyn projects during the '90s. It was worse than being in prison because you knew there was something better out there; you just didn't know how to get it. You never saw green grass or flowers blooming. Instead of looking up to teachers, lawyers or doctors, you worshipped the local drug dealers who hustled to survive and escape their ex istence. Even as a little girl, I knew I wanted more out of life. Somehow hustling was in my blood.

First, I hustled for my moms' attention because she was too busy turning tricks to pay me any mind. I never knew who my daddy was, so while my moms was fucking in her bedroom, I would wait outside the door with my legs crossed, holding my favorite teddy bear in one arm as I sucked my thumb. When the tricks would come out, I would look at them with puppy dog eyes and ask, "Are you my daddy?" The question would freak them out so badly they'd toss me a few dollars so I would shut the fuck up.

One day when I was five, my mother was looking for something in my drawers, she came across a bunch of fives and tens and some twenties. The total was five hundred and some change. Of course, she wanted to know where all the money came from. When I told her that the money came from her business clients (that's what my moms called them), she lit up. She tossed me up in the air and said, "Baby, you my good luck charm. I knew one day you'd make me some money."

On that rare occasion she showed me mad love. As young as I was, I equated my mother's newfound interest in me with love. From that moment on, I learned how to hustle for my moms' attention – that is, by providing her with money.

Where I grew up, everyone hated "The Man," so they wouldn't report shit, even child abuse or neglect. When I was really young, my neighbors helped look out for me, when neces sary. One neighbor, Mr. Duncan, used to babysit me while my mother "Worked." In the projects, we all minded our own business and had the same code of silence that the police have among themselves – we didn't snitch on each other.

Somehow, my moms' customers never messed with or even fondled me. I think it's because people say I got these funny looking eyes. Even when I was little I had an attitude that said, "Don't fuck wit' me."

By the time I was fifteen with all the tricks my moms pulled, we were still dead ass broke, living in the Brooklyn projects. She couldn't save a dime because with hooking comes drugging and my moms stayed high. I guess that's all you can do to escape the nightmare of having all types of nasty, greasy fat motherfuckers pounding your back out every damn day. The characters that I saw coming in and out of our apartment were enough to make me want to sew up my pussy so nobody could get between my legs.

One day when I came home from school, I found my moms sprawled out on the couch with a half empty bottle of whiskey in one hand, as she tried to toke her last pull off a roach in the other hand. Her once long, wavy sandy hair was now thin and straggly. The curves that once made every hood chick roll their eyes in envy were just a bag of bones. You wouldn't even recognize the one time ghetto queen unless you looked into the green eyes she inherited from her mulatto father.

Without a word, I gave the living room a lick and a promise. I emptied several full ashtrays, picked up the dirty glasses scattered about the floor and wiped off the cocktail table. Out of the corner of my eye, I watched my moms sit up and stare at me for a long five minutes. She had the strangest look on her face.

Finally she spoke up. "Precious, you sure are growing up to be a pretty girl." Although we were in each other's face on an everyday basis, it was as if this were the first time my mother had seen me in many years. I didn't know how to respond so I kept cleaning up. "Didn't you hear what yo' mama said?"

"Yes, I heard you."

"Well you betta say thank you." "Thank you, Mama."

"You welcome, baby."

As I continued to clean I couldn't help but feel uncomfortable with the glare my moms was giving me. It was the same look she'd get when she was about to get her hands on some prime dope.

"Baby, you know that your mother is getting up there in age. I can't put it down like I used to."

I looked my moms directly in the eye, but I said nothing. I was thinking to myself, What the fuck that got to do wit' me" "So, baby, I was thinking maybe you need to start helping me out a little more."

"Help out more how, I basically give you my whole paycheck?" I didn't understand what the fuck she was talking about. I barely went to school because I had what was supposed to be a part time job at a car detailing shop.

Damn near every cent I made, I used to pay bills and maintain my appearance. I couldn't afford to rock all the brand name hot shit, but because I had style, I was able to throw a few cheap pieces together to make it look real official. Luckily I inherited my moms' beauty and body so I could just about make a potato sack look sexy.

"Baby, that little job you got ain't bringing home no money. It's just enough to maintain. I'm talking about getting a real job."

"Mama, I'm only fifteen. It's only so many jobs I can get and so much money I can make. Boogie not even suppose to give me all the hours he have me doing at the shop. That's why he pays me under the table."

"Precious, as pretty as you are you can be making thou sands of dollars."

"Doing what? What job you know is going to pay a fif teenyearold high school student thou-sands of dollars?"

"The oldest profession in the booksex," my moms said as if she was asking me to do something as innocent as bak ing cookies for a living.

"You 'un lost your damn mind. What you tryn' to be nowmy pimp?"

"You betta watch yo' mouth, little girl. I'm yo' mama. Don't forget that."

"Don't you forget it. You must have if you ask-ing me to sell my ass so I can take care of you."

"Not meus. Shit, I took care of yo' ass for the last fif teen years. Breaking my back and wearing out my pussy to provide us with a good life."

"This is what you call a good life?" I said as I looked around the small, broke down, two bed-room apartment. The hardwood floors were crack-ing, the walls had holes and the windows didn't even lock. It was nothing to catch a few roaches holding court in the kitchen and living room, or a couple of rats making a dash across the floor.

My moms stood up and started fixing her un-ruly hair, pat ting down her multicolored flannel pajamas and twisting her mouth in that 'how dare you' position as if she were an up standing citizen who was being disrespected in her own home. "You listen here," she began as she pointed her bony finger with its gnawed down nail. "A lot of these children around here don't even have a place to stay. It might not be much but it's mine."

That, too, was a lie. My moms didn't even own this raggedyass apartment; she rented it. But I didn't feel like reminding her of that because I wanted this goingnowhere conversation to be over.

"I hear you, Ma, but I don't know what to tell you. I'm not following in your footsteps by selling my pussy to some low down niggas for money."

"Well then you betta start looking for some place to live, 'cause I can't take care of the both of us."

"You tryna tell me you would put me out on the streets?" "You ain't leaving me a choice, Precious. If you can't bring home some extra money, then I'll have to rent out your bedroom to pay the bills."

"Who is gon' pay you for that piece of shit of a room?" "Listen, I ain't 'bout to sit up here and argue wit' you. Either you start bringing home some more money or find another place to live. It's up to you. But if you don't give me a thousand dollars by the first of the month, I need you out by the second."

With that my moms' skeletal body disappeared into her dungeon of a bedroom. She was practically sentencing me to the homeless shelter.

There was no way I could give her a thousand dollars a month unless I worked twentyfour hours a day, seven days a week at the detail shop. But what made this so fucked up was that my moms basically wanted me to pay for her outofcontrol drug habit. This wasn't even about the bills because our Section 8 rent and other bills totaled no more than four hundred dollars a month. Because the street life had beaten down my moms, she was beating me over the head with bullshit.

With my moms giving me no way out, I began my own hustle. I decided to get the money by selling my ass, but I was going to pick and choose who was able to play between my legs. My job at the car detailing shop came in handy. Nothing but top oftheline hustlers parlayed through, but before, I never gave them the time of day. They were always trying to holla at a sistah, but the shade I gave them was thick.

Boogie, my boss, appreciated that. He was an older dude who took his illegal drug money and opened up his shop. He was in his forties, donned a baldhead and wore two basketball sized diamond studs in each ear. He wore sweat suits and a new fresh pair of sneakers everyday. He could afford any type of car he wanted, but he remained loyal to Cadillac Devilles. He had three: one in red, white and black.

"Boogie, who that nigga in the droptop Beamer?" I asked when some dude I'd never seen before pulled up.

"Oh that's Azar. He moved here from Philly, why you ask?" "I ain't neva seen him 'round here before, and I wanted to know who he was."

"Is that all, Precious?" Boogie asked, knowing it was more than that.

"Actually, to keep it real wit' you Boogie I'm looking for a man."

"What?" Boogie stopped dead in his tracks. "Looking for a man? One of the reasons I digged you so much, Precious, was because you wasn't fucking with none of these hustlers that came through here. Why the sudden change?"

"I'm not gonna get into all that Boogie, but I will tell you I really don't have a choice. I need money and fucking wit' a fosho nigga seems to be the only way to get it."

"Precious, you are much too young to have those types of worries. I could always give you a raise."

"Boogie, unless that raise is a few thousand dollars then it ain't gonna do me no good." Shit, I figured if I had to give my moms a thousand dollars a month, I might as well make a few for me. If I had to sell my ass, then I might as well get top dollar.

"I don't know what you need all that money for, Precious, but if you looking to fuck with a baller, then let me school you on a few things. For one, get your fuck game right."

"What you mean by that?"

"I mean if you want one of these niggas out here to spend some serious paper on you, you gotta learn to sex them real good. You know you're a beautiful girl, so attracting a big timer's attention is the easy part. But to have a nigga willing to spend the way you want, your head and pussy game have to be on point. Just giving you something to think about."

I watched as Boogie went outside to talk to a few guys that just pulled up in G5's. I was still thinking about the advice he gave me. Boogie was right, if I wanted to really land a hustler and keep him, I had to get my fuck game in order. The funny thing was from watching my moms selling her ass all my life, it turned me off from sex. I was probably the last virgin in my hood. I definitely needed a lot of work, and I needed to find someone that I could practice on before I actually went out there and tried to find my baller.

After work I came home and my moms was lying in her regular spot on the dingy couch. She was so bad off that she would've had to pay a nigga to fuck her. I hated to see my moms so broken down. One thing I promised myself was that no matter what, I would never let myself go out like that. I would play niggas; they would never play me.

A KING PRODUCTION

Toxic...

A Titillating Tale

A Novelette

JOY DEJA KING

Chapter One

Got Time Today

"Look at that trifling nigga right there," Harper seethed. "He about to make me fuck my nails up." She glanced down at her freshly done, blush pink mountain peak nails with rhinestone swirls, as her fury continuied to simmer.

"Girl, let's just go. You don't need this drama. You got plenty of other options. You won't have no problem replacing him. Fuck Jamari!" Taliyah was doing her best to get her friend to leave the scene, but it wasn't working. When Harper got amped up, there was nothing nobody could do to lower her temperature.

"Nah, fuck that." Harper's tone had turned calm but icy, which only meant she was about to raise hell. "He ain't about to play me out here in these streets." She grabbed her purse and quickly jumped out her car with Taliyah trailing behind her.

Amina make me so sick! Why the hell did she have to call Harper and let her know Jamari was up in Phipps Plaza shopping wit' the next chick, Taliyah thought to herself as she watched Harper approach her boyfriend.

"What's good?!" Harper popped, sounding more like a dude than the prissy princess her outer appearance exuded. It was the main reason she always had problems with men. They thought they would be dating some submissive eye candy. By the time they realized she had the mindset of a nigga, who just so happened to look good in a dress, it was too late.

"Baby, what you doing here?" Jamari asked nervously, as he was putting shopping bags in the trunk of his car.

"I see you did some shopping. What you buy me?" Harper questioned, grabbing one of the

Louis Vuitton bags.

"Umm, that's mine!" The chick with Jamari shouted trying to snatch the bag out Harper's hand.

"I advise you to let go of this bag, and stay the fuck outta this. This between me and Jamari. You don't want this smoke....I promise you," Harper warned.

The girl didn't know anything about Harper, but her instincts told her the bitch was crazy. So she stepped back, and directed her attention back to the man who had just taken her on a shopping spree. Her first one at that. She didn't want to mess things up with him, but she wasn't trying to scrap in the mall parking lot either.

"Jamari, what's going on...and who is she?" the girl smacked, folding her arms with an attitude.

"Yeah Jamari, who am I?" Harper smirked, enjoying how rattled he was. Although he was trying to act like he had everything under control, his eyes were telling a different story.

"Baby, let me speak to you for a minute." Jamari spoke smoothly, reaching out his hand, and gently taking Harper's arm.

"Get tha fuck off me!" She barked, yanking her arms out his grasp, before pulling out her baby Glock, that she never left home without.

"Yo, yo, yo!" Jamari put his hands up, slowly stepping back.

"I knew that bitch was crazy," the girl who was with Jamari mumbled, shaking her head. Her first thought was to get her phone and call the police, but quickly realized she had already put her purse in the car. She didn't want to draw unwanted attention to herself by opening the passenger door, so she remained in the background quiet.

"Harper, put the gun away and let's go," Taliyah sighed. She was used to her friend's antics but the shit was draining.

"You can go wait in the car for me, 'cause I got time today. We ain't done here, but this won't take much longer," Harper told her friend, keeping her gun aimed at Jamari.

"Baby, please calm down," Jamari pleaded, keeping his hands up. "It's not what you think. You know I love you."

"You so full of shit," Harper laughed wickedly. "It's always you pretty boys that think you can sweet talk yo' way out some lies."

Harper continued to laugh as she began grabbing the pricey items out of the shopping bags. One-by-one, she tossed them in the mud puddles that hadn't dried up from the storm the night before.

"No you fuckin' didn't!" The girl with Jamari screamed. Horrified seeing the luxury goods she envisioned showing off on the Gram being ruined, right in front of her eyes.

"Yo Harper, I can't believe you doing this dumb shit!" He roared, finally losing his cool. Jamari started to storm toward her, until she raised that Glock, aiming it firmly at his chest.

"Back tha fuck up, or else," Harper threatened, nodding her head, tossing out the last bag from the trunk. But she wasn't done yet. She reached back in her purse and brandished the knife she always kept on her too. She proceeded to walk around Jamari's brand new black on black Camaro Coupe ZL1 and slashed each tire.

"You bitch! I'ma fuck you up!" Jamari uttered viciously, ready to break Harper's neck. But she wasn't worried. She was the one holding the gun.

"Ya lovebirds can walk the fuck home, hand in hand. So who's the bitch now," Harper mocked, going back to her car.

"Harper, you are fuckin' certifiable, like seriously," Taliyah kept repeating as she stared back looking at Jamari. He was having a complete meltdown, while the girl he was with, was picking up purses, shoes and clothes, trying to salvage whatever items she could.

"Jamari betta be happy I didn't bust out them windows and key his car too," she snarled. "I bet that nigga learned today not to disrespect me," Harper scoffed, driving off.

Coming Soon... Next In The Toxic Series

Read The Entire Bitch Series in This Order

P.O. Box 912
Collierville, TN 38027

A KING PRODUCTION

www.joydejaking.com
www.twitter.com/joydejaking

ORDER FORM

Name:

Address:

City/State:

Zip:

QUANTITY	TITLES	PRICE	TOTAL
	Bitch	$15.00	
	Bitch Reloaded	$15.00	
	The Bitch Is Back	$15.00	
	Queen Bitch	$15.00	
	Last Bitch Standing	$15.00	
	Superstar	$15.00	
	Ride Wit' Me	$12.00	
	Ride Wit' Me Part 2	$15.00	
	Stackin' Paper	$15.00	
	Trife Life To Lavish	$15.00	
	Trife Life To Lavish II	$15.00	
	Stackin' Paper II	$15.00	
	Rich or Famous	$15.00	
	Rich or Famous Part 2	$15.00	
	Rich or Famous Part 3	$15.00	
	Bitch A New Beginning	$15.00	
	Mafia Princess Part 1	$15.00	
	Mafia Princess Part 2	$15.00	
	Mafia Princess Part 3	$15.00	
	Mafia Princess Part 4	$15.00	
	Mafia Princess Part 5	$15.00	
	Boss Bitch	$15.00	
	Baller Bitches Vol. 1	$15.00	
	Baller Bitches Vol. 2	$15.00	
	Baller Bitches Vol. 3	$15.00	
	Bad Bitch	$15.00	
	Still The Baddest Bitch	$15.00	
	Power	$15.00	
	Power Part 2	$15.00	
	Drake	$15.00	
	Drake Part 2	$15.00	
	Female Hustler	$15.00	
	Female Hustler Part 2	$15.00	
	Female Hustler Part 3	$15.00	
	Female Hustler Part 4	$15.00	
	Female Hustler Part 5	$15.00	
	Female Hustler Part 6	$15.00	
	Princess Fever "Birthday Bash"	$6.00	
	Nico Carter The Men Of The Bitch Series	$15.00	
	Bitch The Beginning Of The End	$15.00	
	Supreme...Men Of The Bitch Series	$15.00	
	Bitch The Final Chapter	$15.00	
	Stackin' Paper III	$15.00	
	Men Of The Bitch Series And The Women Who Love Them	$15.00	
	Coke Like The 80s	$15.00	
	Baller Bitches The Reunion Vol. 4	$15.00	
	Stackin' Paper IV	$15.00	
	The Legacy	$15.00	
	Lovin' Thy Enemy	$15.00	
	Stackin' Paper V	$15.00	
	The Legacy Part 2	$15.00	
	Assassins - Episode 1	$11.00	
	Assassins - Episode 2	$11.00	
	Assassins - Episode 2	$11.00	
	Bitch Chronicles	$40.00	
	So Hood So Rich	$15.00	
	Stackin' Paper VI	$15.00	
	Female Hustler Part 7	$15.00	
	Toxic...	$6.00	
	Stackin' Paper VII	$15.00	
	Sugar Babies...	$9.99	

Shipping/Handling (Via Priority Mail) $8.95 1-3 Books, $16.25 4-7 Books. For 7 or more $21.50.
Total: $_____FORMS OF ACCEPTED PAYMENTS: Certified or government issued checks and money Orders, all mail in orders take 5-7 Business days to be delivered

CPSIA information can be obtained
at www.ICGtesting.com
Printed in the USA
LVHW111639200922
728851LV00004B/632